Baby Du

written by **Jay Dale**

illustrated by Andrew Everitt-Stewart

"Dad," said Bill.
"Can we go
down to the river?"

"We can go down to the river," said Dad.

"We can look for the baby ducks."

Dad looked for the baby ducks.

Bill looked for the baby ducks, too.

"I cannot see the baby ducks," said Bill.

Bill looked in the grass.

Bill looked for the baby ducks.

Dad looked, too.

"Look!" said Dad.

"I can see Mother Duck

in the grass."

"Look!" said Bill.

"I can see the baby ducks, too."